This book belongs to

....

An Imprint of Sterling Published
387 Park Avenue South
New York, NY 10016

SANDY CREEK and the distinctive Sandy Creek logo are trademarks of Barnes and Noble, Inc.

© 2010 by Parragon Books Ltd

This 2011 custom edition is published exclusively for Sandy Creek by Parragon Books.

ISBN 978-1-4351-3750-9

Manufactured in Guangzhou, China
Lot #:
10 9 8 7 6 5 4 3
8/12

The Perfect Snowflake

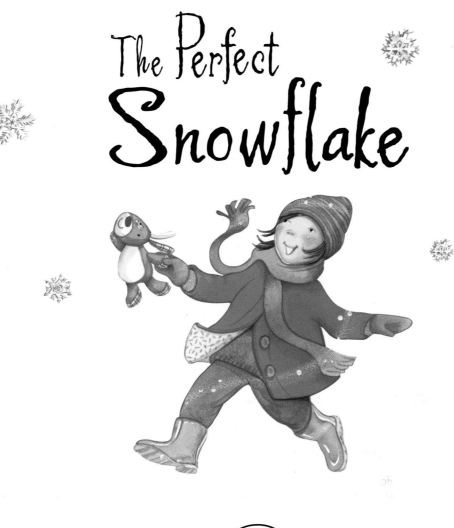

Sandy Creek

One morning, Emma woke up to find
something magical happening outside
her bedroom window.

"It's snowing!" she whispered, excitedly, her warm
breath making misty patterns on the glass.

Outside, snowflakes

swirled and twirled

in the air before floating to the ground.

Emma had never seen anything so beautiful.
"If only I could have a snowflake of my
own to keep!" she thought.

In the yard, Emma caught lots of snowflakes, but each one disappeared when she tried to show Mommy.

"Snowflakes melt when they're warm," Mommy explained.

"But I wanted to keep one!" Emma sighed.

Later that day, the sun shone just as the last few snowflakes fell. They shimmered in the light like sparkly diamonds, before vanishing onto the ground.

That afternoon, Mommy showed Emma
how to make a paper snowflake.

"It's not the same as having a REAL
snowflake," Emma sighed, remembering
what it was like to play in the snow.

"REAL snowflakes dance in the sky."

"REAL snowflakes sparkle in the sun."

"REAL snowflakes **dazzle** like diamonds in the snow!"

Emma couldn't wait to play with REAL snowflakes again.

But the next morning,
when Emma went outside to
play, all the snow had melted.

Just then, the most perfect
snowflake Emma had ever seen
fluttered in the sky.

This snowflake danced in the sky...

sparkled in the sun, and... dazzled like a diamond.

But this snowflake wasn't
real. It was made of paper,
with sparkly sequins and
glitter sprinkled on top.

Emma hugged Mommy.
"This snowflake is
definitely one I can keep,"
she grinned.

How to make Emma's perfect snowflake:

Copy the above pattern onto paper. Ask a grown up to help
you cut out the circle, then fold on the lines, and cut away the
purple areas to reveal your snowflake.